Harry Potter

SLYTHERIN
HOUSE PRIDE

BATSFORD

WIZARDING WORLD

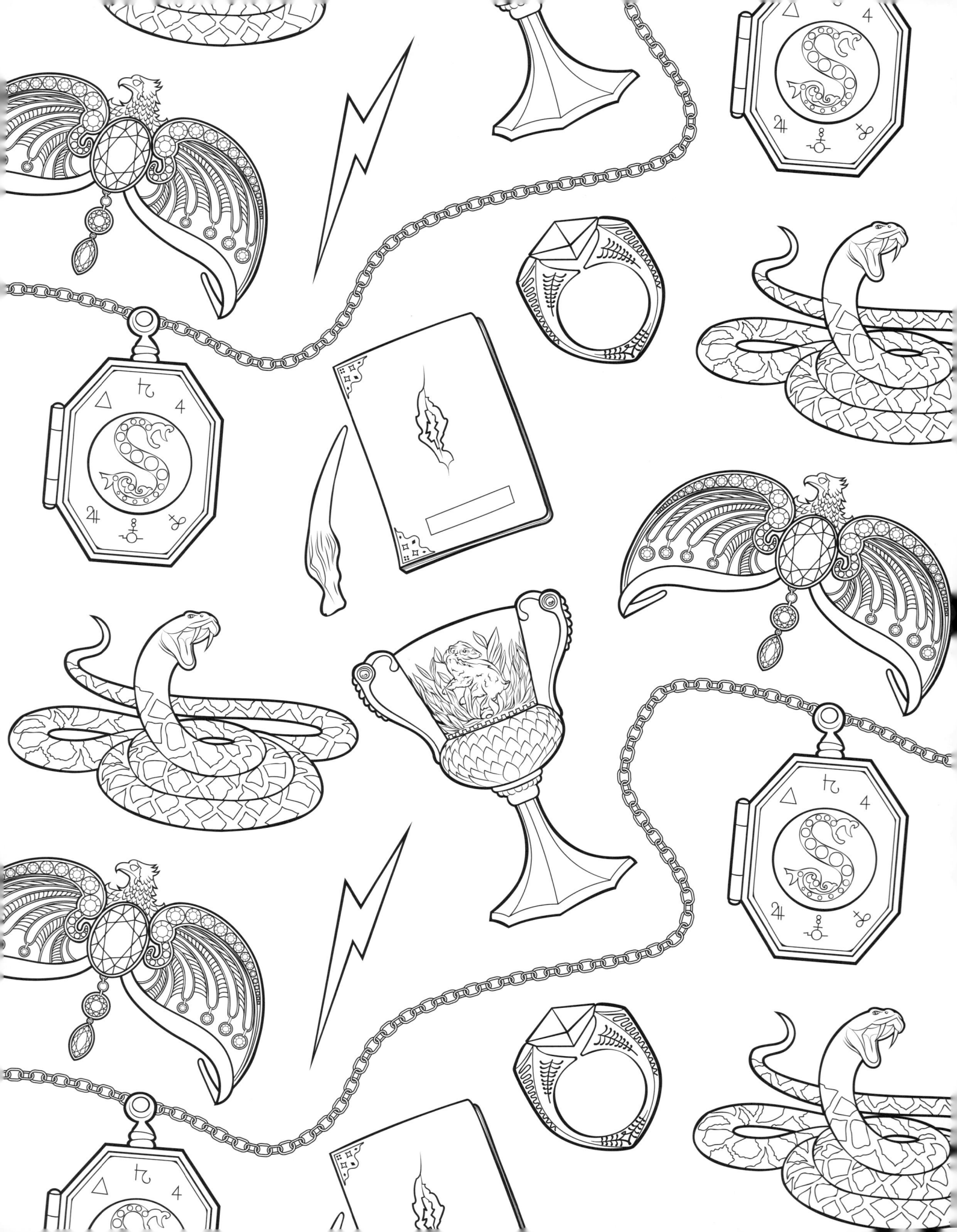

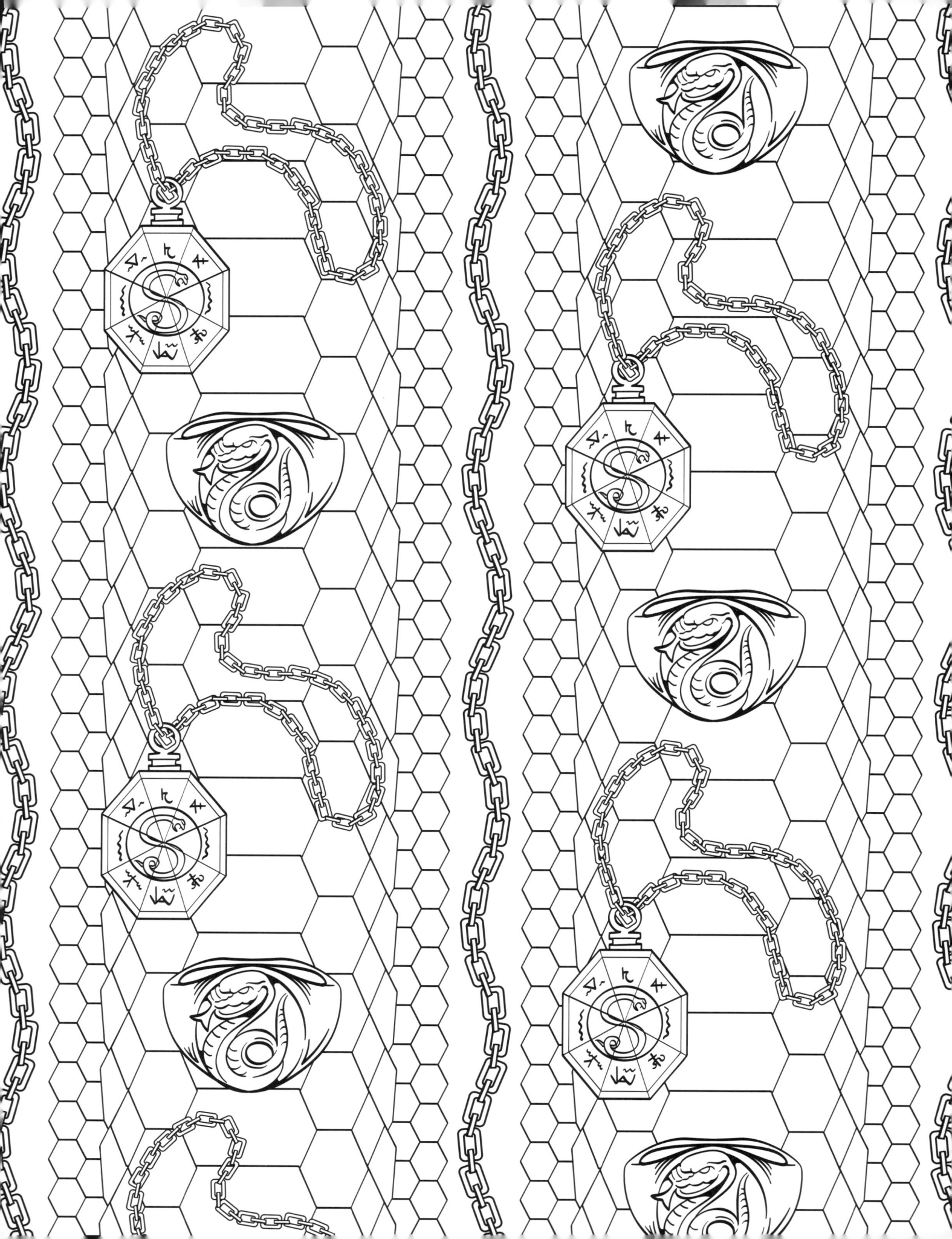

First published in the United Kingdom in 2021 by
B. T. Batsford Ltd
43 Great Ormond Street
London
WC1N 3HZ

Copyright © 2021 Warner Bros. Entertainment Inc. WIZARDING WORLD characters, names and related indicia are © & ™ Warner Bros. Entertainment Inc. WB SHIELD: © & ™ WBEI. Publishing Rights © JKR. (s21)

Published by Insight Editions, San Rafael, California, in 2021. All rights reserved. No part of this book may be reproduced in any form without written permission from the publisher.

ISBN: 9781849947497

A CIP catalogue record for this book is available from the British Library.

10 9 8 7 6 5 4 3 2 1

Publisher: Raoul Goff
VP of Licensing and Partnerships: Vanessa Lopez
VP of Creative: Chrissy Kwasnik
VP of Manufacturing: Alix Nicholaeff
Editorial Director: Vicki Jaeger
Senior Editor: Greg Solano
Design Support: Megan Sinaed-Harris and Monique Narboneta
Associate Editor: Anna Wostenberg
Senior Production Editor: Elaine Ou
Senior Production Manager: Greg Steffen
Senior Production Manager, Subsidiary Rights: Lina s Palma

Thanks to all our artists: Remie Geoffroi, Maxime LeBrun, Pablo Matamoros, Hend_draw from Fiverr, Tomato Farm, Conor Buckley, Paula Hanback, and Iván Fernández Silva

B. T. Batsford Ltd, in association with Roots of Peace, will plant two trees for each tree used in the manufacturing of this book. Roots of Peace is an internationally renowned humanitarian organization dedicated to eradicating land mines worldwide and converting war-torn lands into productive farms and wildlife habitats. Roots of Peace will plant two million fruit and nut trees in Afghanistan and provide farmers there with the skills and support necessary for sustainable land use.

Manufactured in China by Insight Editions